# THE GRAYWOLF SHORT FICTION SERIES

# Free and Compulsory
# for All

Tales by David Romtvedt

Graywolf Press
Port Townsend, Washington
1984

Some of these tales first appeared in the *Crab Creek Review*, and a portion
of this book was originally published as a limited edition chapbook by the
Blue Begonia Press.

Many friends helped in the making of these tales. Thanks to all of them and
especially to Jim Bodeen, Jeanne Crawford, Phyllis Hopeck, Ron Manheimer,
Tad Murdock and Jane Schwab.

*Free and Compulsory for All* received the 1983 Publication Project Award
for Fiction given by the King County Arts Commission, Seattle. The judge
was Jerry Bumpus.

First printing, 1984
2  4  6  8  9  7  5  3

Book design by Tree Swenson
Typesetting by Irish Setter, Portland

ISBN 0-915308-50-9
ISBN 0-915308-51-7 (paperback)
Library of Congress Catalog Number 83-83010

Published by Graywolf Press, Post Office Box 142,
Port Townsend, Washington 98368

Table of Contents

# One

# Two

—For the Schooled

It is the office of the school environment . . . to see to it that each individual gets an opportunity to escape from the limitations of the social group in which he was born, and to come into living contact with a broader environment.

John Dewey
*Democracy and Education*

Most of you, indeed cannot but have been part and parcel of one of those huge mechanical education machines, or mills, as they might more properly be called. They are, I believe, peculiar to our own time and country, and are so organized as to combine as nearly as possible the principal characteristics of the cotton mill and the railroad with those of the model state's prison.

Charles Francis Adams
*address to the National
Education Association, 1880*

. . . to collect little plastic lumps of human dough from private households and shape them on the social kneadingboard.

Edward Ross
*Roots of Crisis*

# One

# Street

A student is walking down a street leading towards a school. Why doesn't the street turn away from the school?

"Why?" asks the student. "For I must follow the street and if only it would turn away I would turn away and follow it somewhere else and not go to school at all."

At school a teacher sees the student and says, "You're late. Why didn't you follow the street faster?" And pushes the student against a wall. Later a second teacher tells the student to close a book, open a door, go into a room. A Biology teacher makes the student breathe formaldehyde and an English teacher feeds the student musty pages from a book of poems.

After the student has been pushed around several times, he begins talking in a loud voice. He screams at the street. And he kicks the street. A piece of it flies up in the air and lands off to the side under a tree. The leaves flutter. This gives the student a good idea. He turns around to follow the street home.

At school a teacher wonders, "Where is my student? When he comes, I'll give him a piece of my mind."

But the student has taken an ax and is standing in the middle of the street hacking at it with all his strength. Pieces of asphalt fly into the air and land under a tree.

# Emerson

After practice, a football player is exhausted. Half asleep, he takes a shower, changes and goes outside to catch a bus home. Staring out the window, he watches the buildings go by— banks, restaurants, real estate offices. The traffic noise is deafening. Still, the motion is hypnotic and he dozes, riding on past his stop.

When he awakens it's to an unfamiliar landscape at the edge of town. A housing project dissolves off into orchards. Grabbing his bundle of things, the player leaps off the bus at the edge of a field. Apple trees as far as he can see. Tired, he walks out and sits down under one. It's not that he's interested in nature. In school he's been told to read Emerson, and as far as he can tell Emerson thinks nature talks to people. The player smiles and leans against the trunk of the tree. The last rays of sun warm his face but the tree doesn't speak. Go ahead, say something, the player thinks. The bus is gone and it is quiet. The player dares the tree to say something. The tree stays silent. As the sun sets the air cools off. So that's it, the player thinks and walks away.

In the dark he tries to find the road, stumbling as he crosses an irrigation ditch. One foot goes down in the water with a great splash. The noise is almost like a voice. Collapsing on the embankment, the player pulls his leg out. As his foot comes up from the mud, there's a feeling of suction. It's like a mouth as it opens and closes.

"Yes?" the player says, and waits. But it only gets colder and the sound stays the same. He gets up, jumps the ditch and walks on, his pant leg dripping. It occurs to him that maybe Emerson was making fun of people when he talked about nature. Asshole, the player thinks.

He follows the ditch until it runs into a conduit to cross a road. On the other side there's a large shed filled with empty apple bins. It's late and there'll be no more buses. So the player slides the tractor-sized door open and looks into the darkness. The wind whistles past the opening, like a person blowing across the top of a bottle. That's a new sound.

"So, you're going to talk to me," the player says to no one. He walks inside and the whistling recedes. With each step it grows darker. He can't see. Reaching the back of the shed, he collides with the wall. His forehead is moist with blood. "Damn," he says, touching it. "Damn, damn, damn," say the corrugated roof and sheet metal walls.

In the morning the player wakes up sore and cold. He shivers. When he gets up he feels dizzy. His first step is a kind of a wobble. Loss of blood? he wonders. With his hand he probes the bump on his forehead. Along one side of his face the blood is dry and caked. I've got to wash and get to school, he thinks, and walks back to the ditch.

Leaning over the water, he sees a muddy brown reflection of himself. He splashes his face and tugs at his matted hair. Water drips from his forehead and his mouth hangs open. It occurs to him that he looks like a bear waking up from hibernation. He looks again. Then, not thinking of Emerson, he plunges his hand into the water and makes a grab at a fish.

# Evening Grosbeaks

So one day a student got up to go to the bathroom and didn't come back. She walked out to where the sky was in full view and looked up. Above her was a flock of birds.

"Evening grosbeaks," she said, and their wingbeats were many small voices saying, "You know some things."

In an orchard the leaves on the apple trees were only tiny suggestions of what they would be. The white blossoms were like popcorn. The girl sat down. As she exhaled, she felt school drain away. At the same time she felt full, like her belly was about to burst.

"There's something in there," she said. And just because a change sometimes helps, she got up and walked on. The wind blew down the grassy way between the apple trees. Petals flew around her head.

"Praise to you for knowing nothing!" the petals shouted.

"What?" the girl said. "Someone else just told me I know some things." The evening grosbeaks flew by. "See," she point-ed. The birds' wingbeats stirred the blossoms, lifting a few al-ready settled ones off the ground.

"Then praise to you for being empty," the petals tried again.

"I don't know about empty, I sure feel full," the girl re-sponded.

"You are full and empty, you know nothing but you know some things, you are the perfect student," the leaves insisted.

"The perfect student out of school," the girl smiled. "Sounds like perfect crap." The wind blew harder and the petals filled the air. It was impossible to see, like trying to walk through a snowstorm. The girl stopped. Petals brushed her skin. So lightly it made her shiver. She turned her face up and stuck out her tongue. A petal landed there. She brought it into her mouth like a child catching a flake of snow. And swallowed.

# Beauty

One lady teacher is very ugly. When she walks by the rugged boy students look away. The pretty girl students cluck at their lockers. Even some of the other teachers make fun of her as they have a beer at the end of the week.

One Monday this ugly teacher comes to school in a very tight blouse with no bra. Everyone sees the perfect round curve of her breasts and the two dark buttons that push their way out. It is all so shocking no one notices the teacher's head has been replaced by the head of a horse, a very ugly horse.

On the second day people do notice and the principal agrees he will have to speak to her. On the third day, though, she is back to normal and he lets it go.

A few weeks later she wears the same tight blouse without the horse's head. The men can't help but look and their eyes show admiration. She wears that blouse for five days in a row, her nipples perfect bullets.

The men are almost used to it when some of the women teachers complain. The principal again sees he must speak to her. Next morning he happens to be walking behind her up the steps. At first he is hypnotized by the sway of her hips. Later he notices she has a bulky knit sweater on. Thank God I won't have to speak, he thinks, and goes into his office tense and relieved.

The ugly teacher, though, has pulled another one. She has attached a milking machine to her two great udders and wears a sign on her milk bag that says "COW." Pretty much everyone agrees something must be done. The Ag teacher says he would like a whole herd of those cows.

Next day the woman is her old ugly self and denies every-thing. She goes so far as to suggest mass hallucination. Now, of course, everyone is watching the ugly teacher all the time. One person keeps a record of her appearance—what kind of clothes she wears and what colors. People notice her shoes and her purse, if she brings a paperback book to school and what she eats for lunch. Soon they are longing for her to wear her horse's head, or take off her bra, or reattach the milking machine. Anything, but not to leave the whole school in suspense.

# Search

A girl is looking for something. She has heard the librarian say she will do a search so the girl looks first in the library. She walks round and round noticing the ferns in the corner and the boy in a cowboy hat reading *Popular Photography*, probably staring at the ads for art photographs.

She looks at the books, passing rack after rack. None seems to hold the book she wants. Angry and impatient, she closes her eyes and extends her hand to the nearest shelf. She pulls down a volume called *The Smell Book*, which tells her that "We communicate with a silent smell language in our bedrooms, dining rooms, offices; in fact, wherever we are, we smell."

Closing the book and looking to see if anyone is watching, the girl remembers the day she farted in class. Though it made no noise and no one said a word, she was sure everyone smelled it. The memory makes her feel offended and ashamed, and she leaves the library promising herself she will never speak to the librarian again.

# Faculty Lounge

Sitting in a room the teachers are cursing at things. One is cursing the moon, which is trying to come through the door but has gotten stuck. Another is cursing the teacher who is cursing the moon. A third, altogether ignorant of the moon, is cursing the bad luck which brought him to be in this room, sitting at a table set with food. Other teachers curse first this then that until the end of lunch when everyone leaves for other rooms. The next day the teachers come back and begin again the cursing, the moon edging through the door.

After some days one teacher ceases to curse, becomes silent, sits for many minutes, head in hands, staring. Wordlessly, he stands and walks toward the door, holding out a hand to the moon. He strokes the moon's powdery skin, tries to put arms around the moon, stretches as far as possible, and still the arms will not reach the dark side of the moon. Perhaps there are cracks between the moon and the doorway, through which one might pass or at least insert an arm. But no, the moon is firmly wedged into the opening.

The teacher steps back and looks at the scene, wanting to squeeze through. Walking to the table and sitting down, he pushes lunch away and begins to curse the shortness of arms.

# Problem

The Home Ec teacher is sitting on a stove. Her legs are crossed and her hands rest on her knee. She lectures on household safety—keeping poisons out of reach of children, installing smoke alarms.... Hearing the word *smoke*, a male student wants a cigarette.

The teacher goes on and the student drifts away, imagining an electric burner on the stove is turned on. It heats up slowly and the teacher keeps talking. After a few moments she wonders why she feels flushed. It comes to her.

"Jesus Christ," she says, leaping to the floor. She grabs the back of her skirt. There's a little fire and the male student rushes forward and beats the flame out with his hands. Red in the face, the teacher thanks him.

As the lecture continues the student realizes he wants to masturbate. He shifts in his chair. Closing his eyes, he pictures himself alone in the room, surrounded by household machines. He walks around, running one hand over the smooth, appliance-white finishes—the cool refrigerator, the blender, the stainless steel sinks and bowls. With his other hand he holds his penis. A little sound comes from his mouth.

The teacher has stopped speaking. The student opens his eyes and sees his fellows turned toward him, smiling. He apologizes. "No need," the teacher says. "Just answer the question." He doesn't know the question. She repeats it: "Imagine you're alone in the Home Ec room. School is over and you're the last one to leave. As you check the room you look out the window. Black clouds fill the sky and you hear thunder. Lightning crashes. The storm rolls closer. Suddenly sparks fly and a toaster explodes. All the toasters explode, bang, bang, bang. The stove begins to vibrate and hum. There are showers of electrici-

11

ty as if small children ran waving sparklers in the air. The stove's electric burners begin to melt, enamel and metal turn to liquid and run along the floor. The linoleum steams. The lights begin to rattle. Maybe the lights fall out of the ceiling and shards of glass rocket around the room. Imagine all this," the teacher repeats. "What do you do?"

All the girls look at the student. Sure he's the only boy in class. But other boys have taken Home Ec. Why pick on him? He realizes that with his hand in his pocket he touches himself. He takes it away and, trying to look at his teacher, admits he doesn't know what to do.

# Headwind

After a department meeting a teacher can only sigh. Remembering what people have said to one another, he walks around the parking lot and, for a few minutes, is unable to find his car. Driving home he encounters a strong headwind. The wind blows the car this way and that. The teacher bucks in his seat. At a stop sign the car keeps going and again the teacher sighs.

"Who is driving this car, me or the wind?" He bangs his hand on the steering wheel. At the next stop sign it is the same. "Well, do what you like," says the teacher. "But one time you won't be so lucky. There'll be a wind coming from another direction and we'll all collide. The police will come and I'll be the one to explain."

The wind keeps blowing and the car rolls through stop sign after stop sign. The teacher takes his hands off the wheel and tries to get some sleep.

# Heartbeat

One night a retired teacher was sitting at home watching television with his wife. In his old age he had moved far out in the country to be away from the lights and nameless young people. The retired teacher got the urge to go outside and take a walk. He told his wife and went to get his coat. He took his flashlight off the shelf and put it in his pocket. Then he stepped out into the night. He looked at the stars and the distant blue-black sky. Taking a deep breath he walked straight away from his house over the brown hills. After a time he turned around and walked back.

When he got near the house he could see a man standing by his car with a large metal can and a rubber hose. The man was siphoning gasoline out of the retired teacher's car. Surprised to see someone so far out in the country, the teacher approached. Standing next to the man he could see it was an ex-student. He took the flashlight out of his pocket and aimed it at the open gas cap to help the other man see. After a time he said, "Please leave me a gallon or two. I have to go to town tomorrow to do errands." The man looked up at the teacher, dropped his hose and began to run away.

"Hey!" the teacher called, waving his light after the running man. "You've forgotten your gas can and rubber hose." But the man only ran faster. The teacher shrugged and turned to go into the house. As he turned he could see his wife standing in the doorway.

"Why, you old fool," she said. "You could have gotten yourself hurt."

"What do you mean?" the retired teacher said. "I had my flashlight."

# Visiting Poet

The visiting poet comes into the classroom. The dark-eyed teacher smiles at him, smiles at the class, smiles at her own dark hands and feet. The poet smiles back at her dark everything. The class smiles into its desks. Smiles so tight that teeth begin to crack.

The poet says, "Imagine a boy in the corner." The class does. "The boy's hands are in his pockets. Now he pulls them out and his fingers flutter, tiny green leaves."

The leaves float around the room. The teacher smiles. The leaves remind her of spring and lovemaking high above a river canyon in a dry meadow. Some students grab for the boy's leaves. Some are stupefied.

"Now imagine the boy wears a hat."

"Fine," everyone says.

"It's a hat made of feathers. Feathers of all colors, violet, chartreuse, blue, pink. Change the colors like a wheel in motion, a wheel rolling down a hill; turn and turn the feathers in the hat."

"How is the boy?"

"He's in the corner."

"But how is he? Is he fine?"

"This is a fine boy," says the teacher.

The feathers begin to droop. The boy puts his hands in his pockets. Feathers cover his face. Only now does anyone notice his dress. Feathers drift down past his shoulders along his small body. They rise from the floor, great mounds of feathers. They climb the body until the boy is buried.

"Where are the boy's clothes?"

"He's naked, he's naked," some say.

At this point the poet speaks directly to the boy: "Hold up

one leg." A leg appears through the feathers. Some students hold their breath as the boy sways in the breeze. "Now lift the other leg," the poet goes on. Out comes that other leg and the boy's head turns on his neck, eyes open.

One student says, "What?"

"Go inside the feathers," the teacher says, and the student does. He's gone. One by one each student disappears into the feather mound under the boy in the corner. One by one they disappear.

"Good," the poet says and looks at the teacher, her dark hair like a flame. "Have the boy lie down. Have him roll across the floor. Have him release flowers—yellow and blue flowers." The boy rolls out the students, each lying flat, each with face up, eyes shut, mouth slack. Each arm is a branch and the fingers silver green leaves quaking in the breeze.

"Good," the poet repeats and goes to the teacher. He puts one hand on her waist, one hand on the back of her neck. He opens his mouth and asks the boy in the corner to sing. The boy sings. The poet and the dark-eyed teacher kiss. The students breathe evenly. Feathers fill the room.

# Dust

On Monday there's a note in the Art teacher's box. The principal would like to see him if he has a minute. What now, the Art teacher wonders. When his preparation period comes, he goes to the office. The principal's out but he'll be right back. The Art teacher waits, noticing little bits of clay that have fallen off his shoes onto the floor. He's aware that some people don't like it that he's always covered with clay and paint and dust. He crosses his legs and more clay falls to the floor. He finds himself doodling on the bench with a soft lead pencil. He tries to joke with the secretary but she won't joke back. The student assistant smiles at him. He smiles at her. Neither can trust the other.

The Art teacher begins tapping his shoes with his pencil. More clay falls to the floor. He really is kind of messy. He tries to brush off his shirt. Dust flies. The principal sweeps into the room. The Art teacher stands, trying to shake hands and brush off his pants at the same time. More dust flies. The room's incandescent light filters through the particles. The air is filling up.

"Ah," the principal says, and with his arm makes a sweeping gesture toward his office. Then he changes his mind. "Ahhhh, chooo," he says. His body jerks, his chin momentarily touches his chest as his head snaps forward. His right foot lifts off the ground and comes back down. A little pool of settled dust rises.

It's like a dance, the Art teacher thinks, a Navajo dance—the arm's sweeping arc, the head thrown back then forward, the foot as it stamps the floor. The Art teacher turns, repeats the gestures and smiles. The principal seems to smile back or maybe is preparing another sneeze.

"Look at this," the Art teacher says to the student assistant. His foot slaps the floor and another pool of dust floats upward.

Now the student assistant smiles, really smiles. She throws back her head and shakes her brown hair free. It falls, cascading. She spins and the long flying hair gathers dust from the air. Somehow, even through the dust, everything shines. The student's feet rise and fall on the earth. There's no floor left, just red dust on red earth, the yellow sun in the sky. She dances, naked feet on the ground. The Art teacher dances along with her. The principal continues to sneeze.

# Sex Education

Parents have to sign a permission slip for their children to attend and class is held in the evening. Boys go one night, girls another. On the boys' night, everyone files into the cafeteria for the lecture. The cafeteria smells of milk and disinfectant. The man who lectures uses the empty salad bar as a lectern. He peers over the cash register. It's a little like a doctor's examining room, all those empty stainless steel trays usually filled with vegetables and cheese, sunflower seeds and dressings. Only now they're empty.

The teacher puts down his notes and visual aids. He's got transparent models of different parts of the body—the head, the heart, the midsection, the genitalia. When he sets it down, the head rolls into the lettuce tray. The heart rests where tomorrow there will be ranch dressing. The midsection stands facing the students.

It is very quiet in the room as the teacher picks up the transparent genitalia, a disembodied penis and testicles supported by a steel rod and mounted on a wooden base. There is a nylon string in the rod and a hinge on the penis. When the teacher pulls the string down, the penis lifts up on the hinge.

The teacher begins to explain an erection. Like a tick, he pulls on the string so the penis goes up and down as he talks. That swinging penis looks like a railroad warning gate gone crazy. The teacher mentions sebaceous glands that secrete a substance of very peculiar odor. The students hear about the integument, the erectile tissue, the corpora cavernosa and the arteries, branches and capillary network. It's not very sexy. Matter of fact, it's unpleasant. Some students say the teacher is a sicko, the plastic penis bobbing up and down.

Before discussing the testes, the teacher explains surgical

anatomy of the region. He says the penis occasionally requires removal for malignant disease. If this becomes necessary, the operation can be performed by cutting off the whole of the anterior part with one sweep of the knife. The teacher makes the sweeping gesture with his left hand and the next moment stands holding the severed penis like a cucumber in his right. In the room there is an audible gasp. The teacher laughs and reassembles his model. It's a joke. He's a jerk, some students think. The rest of the evening is uneventful.

Riding home on his bicycle, it occurs to one student that though he's never thought of it before, his penis is in the way. And the narrow seat slices into his testicles like a dull knife. As the days go by it proves impossible to shake this feeling.

Next week he rides to his second Sex Education class. This time he hears about the mons veneris, the labia majora and minora, the clitoris, the meatus urinarius and the orifice of the vagina. The teacher again shows transparent models but plays no tricks. Riding home the student notices the beam his bike light throws onto the road. There preceding him lies a pattern of light and dark that looks like a vagina, the light's hesitant rings around a narrow vertical opening. The student switches off the light and rides the dark familiar street home. Concerned not to fall in a pothole or hit a curb, he forgets the week-long discomfort in his crotch.

# What Matters

A woman took off all her clothes and ran through the school. She always wore a mask so it was impossible to tell who she was. She might have been a student. Or a younger teacher. Or a clerk in the office. She might even have been someone not connected to school at all—a prankster trying to liven up the scene.

She ran through naked at least once a week but never at the same time nor in the same place. One Wednesday she ran through Auto Shop just as they fired up all the motors. She ran through Contemporary World Problems. She ran through an English Department meeting in the middle of a conversation on what to include in the curriculum. She ran through the mandatory school Christmas assembly. She ran through the sophomore boys' shower room after PE—an agonizing delight. She was pretty fast. The only time she slowed down was when she ran through Art class. The Art teacher always waved and smiled and when he saw her coming he'd yell to his class, "Okay, get ready for a quick figure study." She took to waving back.

They tried to catch her but she always seemed to have an escape planned—a waiting car or a quick disappearance down a little-used alley. In winter it got to be too much: her erect nipples and the rosy cast to her skin. An all-school assembly was called to address the problem. Students must not get the idea that they can get away with something in life. In the middle of the principal's prepared lecture, the Art teacher leapt up and called out, "There's only one thing that matters. Only one thing." Everyone turned, wondering if this was part of the program, or what it could be that matters. "When she runs through here, legs turning and flesh flying, which is rounder, her left buttock? Or her right? And which is longer, her great toe? Or her second?"

For a few moments there was a large silence. Then the principal began to laugh. "Oh, that Art teacher, always making jokes." So everyone laughed. But there was one student who knew the answers to those questions. He didn't speak, but next term he signed up for Art.

# Blind

To start practice the coach has all the players shoot free-throws. "Free-throw percentage can mean the difference between winning and losing," he likes to remind his players. That's okay, it's kind of fun shooting free-throws.

One student, though a good player, couldn't make those free-throws. He'd step to the line, take aim and miss. And miss. And miss again. One day of a hundred free-throws he made eleven. It was kind of eerie when Coach walked up to him and said, "You'd be better off blind you know, make more than that by chance."

"You're probably right," the student player said, and instead of running through practice, went home. Next day he returned to practice wearing thick dark glasses and carrying a white cane tipped in red. He banged his way through the doors, tapping the floor and wall. He tapped his way onto the parquet court, the sound echoing around the gym. At first everyone ignored him. Then they said okay okay good joke. But he kept walking—bouncing off the empty officials' table, scraping his shins on the first row of bleachers. How did he get his locker open to put on his uniform, someone wondered.

Finally another player took him by the shoulders and led him up to the free-throw line. He gave the blind player a ball and said, "Shoot. The basket's straight in front of you."

And the blind player shot 6 for 10. Amid applause and laughter he shot again—5 for 10. Not good, but better than yesterday when he was sighted. Coach came over and the blind player went 8 for 10. This time Coach himself retrieved the ball after each shot—6 for 10. The player in the polarized glasses had shot 25 for 40. Over 60 percent.

"Impossible," Coach said, but he had the player go on, and

out of 100 shots he made 63. Blind. "Now you've got it," Coach shouted, beginning to understand.

The student took off his dark glasses and blinked, squinting in the light. "I really made 63? Guess I am better off blind, huh?"

But Coach, angry to see the student's open eyes, shoved the dark glasses back in place. "Blind men can't see," he said. "Now get out there and learn to pass."

# Cheerleader

"I'm a cheerleader," a girl says to herself. "I'm actually rising in the air in the middle of a jump and hundreds of people are shouting because of me."

She comes down with a thud. Her clean white tennis shoes squeak on the hardwood floor. It's a seesaw game. The lead changes hands as often as the ball. The boys run up and down the court. They sweat and pant. There's a foul. A boy steps to the line in silence. Everyone holding their breath, you can hear only the boy, the air drawn into his lungs and pushed back out. The ball drops through the net and there's a thunderstorm of screams. The cheerleaders bounce up and down. They face the fans, then the players. They're everywhere at once, urging everyone on: "Hurry, hurry!"

In the middle of the last quarter this one cheerleader notices an ant walking across the floor. It's crossing the gym at midcourt. Fast break. Twenty feet crashing down-court. The cheerleader's heart is in her throat. When she looks again she sees the ant is still moving, miraculously untrampled. But here come the twenty feet again. And again the ant survives. The cheerleader smiles and says a silent cheer for the tiny player. In spite of the continuing passage of feet the ant reaches the other side.

"He's made it!" the cheerleader shouts and everyone looks at her in a quizzical way. What does she mean he's made it? No one even shot. She smiles sheepishly and waves. "Go," she says, and thinks maybe that ant isn't male at all. Could be a girl ant that made it across the basketball court.

Finally the game ends. At home her father asks, "What was the score?" But she can't remember. "You can't remember?"

25

he says. "Well, who won?" She thinks hard but can't remember that either. Her father is incredulous and suggests she keep her mind on the game and off the boys who are playing it. They both have a good laugh and she kisses her father good night.

# No, No, No

There was a student who couldn't keep herself from changing. She'd wake up in the morning and go fearfully to the mirror to see what night had brought. Once she found a long red scar down the side of her face and had to comb her hair across it. "Love your new do," a girlfriend called out at school. Another time one of her breasts expanded like a balloon filled with water. She lifted it with one hand. It weighed a ton. Her hand was a crab's claw. She had to even herself out, wear several layers of shirts, an old baggy sweater and a pair of wool mittens. "Dontcha know it's spring?" her boyfriend asked, wondering what she was trying to hide.

It never seemed to stop. Her nose migrated down to her neck, her feet got turned around backwards. Her hair turned white. Thank God nothing lasted long and she'd never changed all at once all over. She'd never found herself turned into a horse, say, or worse, into a bale of hay.

But one day she woke up with a metronome instead of a head. Clic, clac, clic, clac, she went. No one could tell if she was making fun of them. She measured sixty beats per minute in perfect time with the clock. Everyone watched and listened. Everyone waited for release. It is normal enough for students to watch the clock, the teachers thought, but this is almost arrogant. So they said she had undermined order and had her transferred to a special classroom. There she turned into a goldfish and was flopping about on her former desktop near death when a boy drinking a soda scooped her up and put her in his mouth, thus allowing her to breathe.

# Custom

There is an old custom that after work when a man comes home again to his wife he throws his hat in the door and waits a few minutes. If the hat stays inside then the man can go in. If the hat comes flying back out then the man can take a walk.

There's a teacher who does this at school. Each day he comes five minutes late to class. He opens the door and throws in the textbook. It always comes sailing back out. So the teacher walks back to the faculty lounge and wonders what the students do for the hour alone there in the room.

After many weeks of this the teacher tries something different. He throws in a copy of *War and Peace*. Out it comes. But it takes a few minutes. That's heartening. The next day he tries the *Pictorial World Atlas*. It too is returned, this time with a note that reads, "Some of us enjoyed the mineral deposits maps." Warmed by this second positive response the teacher throws in *The Use and Abuse of Art*. It comes back even faster than the textbook. The teacher is rattled now and throws in a copy of *Playboy* magazine. A long time goes by. He's just about to enter the classroom when out flies the magazine. It nicks the teacher's ear and comes to rest on the floor, opened to the playmate of the month, Miss Sherry Sweet.

He picks up the magazine and goes back to the lounge where he reads an interview with a famous rock'n'roll musician who says "All we are saying is what is happening to us. We are sending postcards. It isn't that we are awakened and you are sheep that will be shown the way. That's the danger of saying anything, you know." The teacher reads that twice. Then he reads that the famous musician was recently killed by a crazed assassin. He reads it a third time: ". . . the danger of saying anything." People will think you are telling them what they ought to think. He thinks he can see what he's been doing wrong with his class.

The next day he goes to his room at the proper time and confidently enters. He reads the musician's statement to his students. He smiles, sure they will smile too. They don't. They don't frown. They just don't do anything. When the bell rings they get up and leave the room without speaking. Next day not one student shows up for class. The teacher wonders if he should throw a book out into the hall.

# Communication

One day the Art teacher has had enough. A famous artist is in town for a show and he has agreed to visit a class. He brings slides of his work and one painting which looks to the students like a giant paramecium suspended in Chinese alphabet soup.

"The Chinese don't even have an alphabet," a student whispers.

The famous artist mentions Magritte and Miró, Matisse and Braque. When he says Kandinsky, a student calls out "Sure can!" And another says "Gezundheit." One girl wants to know why all famous artists are men. In the middle of the laughter the intercom starts to hum, and a voice asks some student to report to the nurse and tells some teacher to phone his wife. It makes the Art teacher mad, all day these interruptions, every day—the morning bulletin, the afternoon activity news, unannounced pleas for aid from some organization that's selling chocolate whatnots to support the Lion's Club cornea transplant program.

When the intercom goes off the famous artist goes on. He tells how he became a painter against the wishes of his mother and father, who wanted him to be a dentist. "I couldn't imagine myself a dentist," he laughs, "peering into all those wet dark mouths, pulling teeth out of people's heads. . . ."

The students are warming up to him and laugh at this vision of the famous artist as a dentist. Then the intercom comes back on. The famous artist stops. The Art teacher picks up a pair of grozzing pliers, opens the intercom box and, clamping the pliers onto the wires, rips them out of the wall. There's a brief crackle followed by silence. The students have the good manners to applaud.

# Presidential Visit

The auditorium was built a long time ago. It's the color of dust. Everything at this school is the color of dust. Except dust. Dust is gray.

Herbert Hoover came to dedicate the auditorium. Actually, Herbert Hoover never came here. It was a local clown dressed up in an old-time suit, wearing a Herbert Hoover mask. That was in 1965. And the clown had a heart attack in the middle of the dedication. The paramedics rushed through the gray dust but couldn't get the mask off so did nothing. When the clown came around on his own he believed he really was Herbert Hoover and began to recite one of his campaign speeches. Only he remembered incorrectly and gave a speech originally delivered by Calvin Coolidge.

# A Play

They're giving a play. A woman in the play is dancing with a cat, a female cat. The dance is a samba. Another cat is nursing a litter of little girls. The little girls close their eyes and push their cupped hands against the mommy cat's belly. A woman is eating cat ovary soup and saying "ahhh, mmmmm, yes, ahhh," and blowing across her spoon. Because it's a play she doesn't actually swallow any. The last woman stands under a lamp post meowing at a cat who is lecturing on Kierkegaard's wife's cooking. Did Kierkegaard have a wife?

"This play is great!" some students say. Some teachers, too. But some students say they don't understand the play. And some teachers say there's nothing to understand, it's just stupid. The principal wonders, "How come all the actresses are women?" and "How did they train all those cats?"

# Parade

Class is going on as usual when a policeman appears wearing a dark blue uniform with tarnished metal buttons. He begins to explain the derivation of the word "copper," rubbing his buttons with a greasy rag. His hat has a round top that slopes back from the front, ending in a black visor. Above the visor is his badge, with surname and department number. The badge also says "Cleveland Police." This is odd, since the school isn't in Cleveland. It isn't even in Ohio.

The policeman suggests everyone pretend to be a parade. The students line up and begin walking in a circle around the desks. The policeman is last in line. It's then that he takes out his gun and strikes a student over the head. The student falls, but the line spreads out and fills the gap. The policeman strikes a second student. And a third. There's no stopping him. Soon the students litter the floor. The policeman keeps the parade going but now must pick his way along, lifting his feet so as not to crush the silent faces.

The teacher, aghast at her inactivity, sits. Exerting all her will, she shouts at the policeman to stop. He turns and smiles in recognition. "I know you," he says. "We grew up together in Cleveland."

# Discovery

The Physics teacher was a nice man, but Physics was so difficult and so boring. One day a student fell asleep in class. He sat way in the back and the teacher might never have known but that suddenly the student fell out of his desk and landed on the floor with a clunk. He lay sprawled in the aisle, snoring. Other students had tried to catch him, but to no avail. Now it was too late. The teacher stopped his lecture, held his index finger to his lips and said, "Shhhh."

With the help of the other students he made a bed of coats and laid the sleeping student in the back of the room. Then he told the students who were still awake that "no great physical discovery has been made without a lot of dreaming beforehand," and he went on with his lecture. Some students listened twice as hard now, though others were as bored as ever.

# Dactyl

In order to pass the section on poetry in junior English, the students must identify the various metrical feet used in English verse—the iamb and the trochee, the anapest and the dactyl. It's hard for the students to get these feet straight, and it's hard for the teacher too. He never could remember them all, has to keep looking them up and repeating the definitions to himself.

Finally he hits on a trick and explains it like this: "The dactyl is a metrical foot of three syllables, one accented syllable followed by two unaccented ones. The word 'dactyl' is Greek and literally means 'finger.'"

The teacher holds his right hand up and extends his index finger. It looks like he's got a gun with which he's trying to shoot himself in the head, but he's going to miss.

"The word 'dactyl' is used because the foot has three syllables, like the finger has three joints, and the first syllable is the longest, just like the finger's first joint." The teacher smiles and turns to the class.

"Don't point that finger at me," someone shouts, "it might be loaded." Laughter.

The teacher says, "Okay, everybody got it?" And he asks a student to explain this metrical foot. The student lifts his closed hand and extends his middle finger straight up in the air.

"Dactyl you, man," he says. Almost everyone laughs. The teacher is momentarily angry but realizes the truth is the student got the answer right.

# The Ongoingness

Some students say of one teacher that he looks like a chicken on roller skates. And when he opens his mouth to speak the sound that issues forth is like a whale trying to pass for a ferry boat.

But there is this: he's never missed a day of school. Matter of fact he keeps going all summer. He's got a camp chair he carries on his back and a thermos bottle he fills with tepid tomato soup. When he arrives in front of his locked room he removes his watch and carefully sets it on the ground in front of himself as do all the professors when they begin a lecture. All morning the teacher waits and watches. No one comes by because it's summer. Well, once in a while a grade school kid who says, "Hi!" and asks what's happening. The teacher sets off into the periodic table of elements. At noon he sighs and opens his thermos. He notices he's forgotten a spoon and reseals the thermos. He considers it vulgar to drink soup from a cup. In the afternoon he listens to his stomach grumble and hopes tomorrow he will bring a spoon. At 3:30 he folds his camp chair up and goes home.

His wife says the air is getting cooler. Soon it'll be fall. She doesn't believe him when he tells her about class that day.

# Sunday Service

One of the teachers invites her class to service at the church. This Sunday the minister's talk will be on what public schools do to the minds of our youth. The teacher promises that everyone who comes will get a half grade extra credit.

On Sunday morning as the students enter the church with the rest of the parishioners, the minister greets them at the door wearing a black cap and gown, a white shirt and a striped tie. He tells everyone to sit down in the vestibule and wait until he gives permission to enter the sanctuary.

"And sit down in rows according to height," he asks.

The people giggle but they figure out who is tallest and who shortest and they sit down in order. Waiting there, they can hear the minister in the sanctuary. It sounds like he is pushing heavy boxes around on the floor.

"What's going on? It's past time for the service to start," a man whispers. "Maybe something has gone wrong."

The minister comes back smiling and invites everyone in.

"Don't forget your order," he reminds them and rises to the pulpit. When everyone is seated, he begins. As he speaks he becomes animated and loosens his tie. He takes it off. A few minutes later, he takes off his cap and gown. Continuing, he undoes the top button on his shirt, the second and the third. He drops the shirt on the floor next to the pulpit. He bends over and disappears. His left shoe flies out and lands on the organ keyboard. The chord it plays sounds like D Minor. The right shoe lands on the floor with a clunk. The minister reappears, still talking. He's doing something with his hands. As he pauses, the congregation can hear his zipper move. His belt buckle makes a metallic noise when his slacks land at his feet. He gesticulates as he speaks.

"Now," the minister says, "I want the visiting students to move to the aisles and be row monitors. Make sure no one in your row speaks or moves until I come back and give the signal." With that the minister steps out from behind the pulpit. Completely naked, he walks past the congregation and out the door. Nobody turns a head. For a little while after he's gone nobody moves. Some people can't help but remember how his penis hung slightly to one side. Others are amazed that he moved like a man fully clothed.

The minutes tick by. The whispers begin.

"I don't think he's coming back."

"Do you think he's coming back?"

"He's got to get his clothes."

"I don't think he's coming back."

The row monitors are nervous. They realize they've been here before and aren't sure when to let people get up and leave.

# Two

# Rain

It is raining. The Biology teacher has finished for the day—
dissecting frogs. How many frogs he has had students cut up
and examine, naming the parts. And earthworms and fetal pigs.
He can show students how to separate an animal's brain from
its central nervous system. Part is dead and part behaves as
though it goes on living. This helps students to learn.

When the Biology teacher steps out of the building after having been indoors all day, he is surprised to see the wet streets
and the rain. Driving home he notices hundreds, maybe thousands of frogs coming up off the shoulders and hopping across
the roadway. He hits one. He can feel the crunch of small bones
under the left front tire. It comes up through the steering wheel
as clear as if he'd stepped on it or crushed it in his hand.

Now he can't seem to avoid the frogs. He tries swerving and
braking but it's no good. He hits another frog and swerves more
violently. Other drivers honk and try to get out of his way. They
shout curses at this crazy driver but their voices are muted by
soft rain. Nothing the Biology teacher does helps. He hits a third
frog. He is swerving and shouting curses now, too.

Finally he arrives home, unable to say how many frogs he has
killed. He pulls into the garage and turns the motor off but it
continues to sputter along on its own. He gets out of the car and
opens the hood, bangs his hand on the fender, speaking bitterly
about his work, about frogs, about other people, and about
technology. About this last he speaks most bitterly of all. He
looks at the motor still trying to turn itself over. Stop it, he thinks,
and pulls the cable off the end of a spark plug. A blue flash leaps

out of the wire. The shock runs through his hand into his arm. Shouting, he holds the hand up in the air. The fingers quiver and twitch.

Now the motor is off and the Biology teacher goes in the house, wanting only to rest.

# Popularity

A man was a teacher. Most of all in life he wanted to protect himself from the young. Looking at them he saw a power that was brutal and blind. He could not believe he was like that in youth. His inclination was to hide himself from the young—to be a hermit in some far cave or the activities director of a retirement community. But he knew if he did either it would only be worse. Some young couple would stumble drunk into his cave wanting to pull at each other's flesh, or some grandchild would unexpectedly come to visit its grandparent. Unprepared for these shocks, he might lash out, scream, or worse, strike a young person.

It occurred to him that his best preparation was to look his fear in the eye. Walk through fear, he thought. So he had become a schoolteacher. He gave interesting lectures and answered students' questions with a directness that surprised them, surprised even himself. They knew he didn't like them but they liked him. Maybe the hate is a big act, some students said. Maybe he's shy or afraid of us. There was even a rumor he'd been fired from his last job because he was a homosexual and had been caught with a running back from the football team.

Whatever the truth, students came to like this distant teacher. They'd try to talk to him after school as he ran for his car. They asked him to be the faculty sponsor for their clubs. They went to his house on Saturdays. He gave them cokes and, infrequently, glasses of beer. They talked. As he kept silent, they thought he listened. Really he counted the minutes, waiting for them to go.

# Popularity (Two)

There was a fat girl. Not only was she fat but she was ugly. Her eyes were two tiny seeds planted in the puffy discolored field of her face. Her lips were the scarred banks of a murky irrigation ditch. Her nose was a cauliflower floweret. There was nothing good-looking about her. Maybe philosophically ugliness is beautiful and maybe a beautiful representation of an ugly thing can please the eye, but in school philosophy is bunk. She was not popular.

There was a boy who looked very ordinary. He might not be in the popular crowd but nothing about him indicated that he should be outcast. Except for one thing. The ordinary boy's one problem was that he thought he might be homosexual. Many of his classmates were sure he was. When he walked he set his foot down flat then rocked forward onto his toes to take another step. That was a sure sign.

The fat girl and the ordinary boy ran around with a few other students, mostly fat or ugly or peculiar. After knowing each other for over three terms, the fat girl and the ordinary boy began to talk of their problems.

"The fear of the body," he said, running his hand through his hair.

"What we are meant to be," she replied, looking at her feet. The girl had never been touched by a boy; the boy had never tried to touch a girl. They began to go out, just the two of them. They stayed away from talk of aesthetics, going to baseball games, movies, for walks along the river. That's what they mostly did—walk along the river in full view of the other walkers. Everyone stared.

Just to find out they began to kiss goodnight. He pressed himself against her. She felt his heartbeat through all her layers.

One night she invited him in. They sat on the couch in the dark and made out. He began to unbutton her blouse. She moved to stop him, then realized this was why they'd begun—to find out. He put his hand inside the blouse, reached around and unsnapped her bra. She gasped. Her breasts fell like water rushing free when a dam breaks. She felt ashamed, then proud. This was herself, this mound of soft flesh, larger than anything he'd ever seen. She arched her back, lifted a breast with one hand and pulled him toward her with the other. When he came close, she could feel him getting hard.

After a time they stopped and the boy went home. That was the end. He wasn't any surer than before. And she didn't feel different. They kept going out for walks but never spoke of their night. What could come of a possibly homosexual ordinary boy and a fat ugly girl?

# Kept After School

Two students are being punished by being made to sit silently together in a room. The teacher who must stay after school to watch them goes out in the hall and stands behind the door waiting to see if the students speak. But the students know the trick, and use only hand signals. Pleased by the silence the teacher returns and releases the students fifteen minutes early. At the corner they turn in opposite directions toward home. One walks with his girlfriend.

"What happened at detention?" she asks.

"When the teacher went outside the room we made a funny joke. I held up one finger like we used to in grade school when we had to pee. The other fellow held up two fingers like when we had to poop. We both kept straight faces, knowing we'd be in trouble if we laughed aloud. Then I held up three fingers to say the teacher was probably pooping and peeing at the same time. Finally, the other fellow made a fist and turned it round and round like the teacher's head going down the toilet. Before I could think what to do next the teacher came back in and we got out early for being quiet."

"Pretty neat trick," his girlfriend says.

The other student had already arrived home. His father asked why he was late. He explained about the punishment. He apologized. He told about the silent conversation.

"The other fellow knew we weren't supposed to talk but when the teacher left the room he held up one finger to show we could say one word without getting caught. I held up two fingers to show that if we did get caught we'd have to stay twice as long. Then he held up three fingers to let me know he was going to say three words and maybe we would get caught and I shouldn't be such a goody-goody. I thought about that and

46

made a fist to show that if he said anything I'd fight with him when we finally did get out. Before he could answer the teacher came back in and let us go early. I guess it pays to be tough sometimes."

"Yes," the father said, "sometimes there's no other way."

# Innovative Assignment

One day a teacher says, "No class today. Go outside and walk around. Maybe go to the lounge and listen to the pinball machine or go sit in another class and see how it feels. Whatever you do, think about your feelings. If you're bored or depressed or sad or angry or shameful or anxious or even happy, why? Think your feelings through. Do it all day. Tomorrow come back to class and we'll talk about it."

"That's a funny assignment," a girl whispers to a boy as they leave hand in hand.

"But how do you feel?" he says and smiles. She rolls her eyes and squeezes his hand.

Next day in class the teacher stands by his desk without speaking. The students chat and laugh. One coughs. Thinking this is a cue to begin, everyone becomes quiet.

"Well," the teacher says. Everyone waits. The boy and girl who are sweethearts look at each other. Silence. Then the boy starts:

I went out on the walkway around the building. The wind was blowing. I could see little bits of paper and old snow blowing across the ice in the courtyard. I enjoyed that but I was angry. I thought this is a stupid way to teach school. If my dad found out I was wandering around not even in class he'd call the principal. He'd say it's no wonder I don't know anything. I stuck my hands in my pockets and paced around. I'd left my hat in the room but I wasn't going back so my head was cold. I walked away from school toward the park. I wished I was with my girlfriend . . .

The word girlfriend hangs there in the air and some students look up.

I got to the park where I walked across the baseball diamond. It was covered by dirty snow. My boot came down on the untracked crust. There was a slight hesitation then the crust broke and the boot fell through. I ran slowly around the diamond like a player who hit a homerun. It was warm; I unzipped my jacket. It felt like I was running straight into summer. . . .

Sitting in his chair, the teacher is reeling. This is better than anything he could have hoped for. These are some students. He stops the boy but before he can speak the girl begins:

I thought about my boyfriend. I closed my eyes and saw his face. I touched his cheek. That made me feel both good and bad. We've been going steady a long time. Sometimes I wonder what I've missed. When I see him I smile and forget what I may have missed. And I forget how boring my classes are. I forget about men teachers who look at my breasts then go in the teachers' lounge and talk about how kids have nothing on their minds but sex. My boyfriend and I started sleeping together this term. We're careful. I haven't told my mother. I've got a diaphragm and he always uses a condom. My mother'd call me a slut. Last night walking home in the dark I started to cry. The tears ran down my cheeks. It was so cold the tears burned. Then they froze. I thought about that. Frozen tears like those tears will always be there no matter where I go or what I do. Whether I marry my boyfriend or go to college or have kids. Always the tears. . . .

The teacher himself is frozen. The girl has stopped but he can't remember when. And he isn't sure what was the last thing she said. The class looks at the girl. Then at her boyfriend. Then at the teacher who still hasn't said a word.

On the side of the room a hand goes tentatively up in the air. It waves, like a leaf of bamboo in a wind. The teacher shudders and forces himself to respond.

"Yes?" he says.

"What about you?" the student asks. "How do you feel?"

49

# Crowd

Everywhere and always the pushing and pulling and leaning. The buses pull up in the morning and their packed contents spill out like so many herring being flipped out on the deck of a boat, silver scales blinding in the sun. During the warm parts of the year there's hanging out in the courtyard. When it's cold, the students go straight to the classrooms and into chairs amid squeaking and scraping and scratch of clothes.

At lunch there are three shifts and the cafeteria's always full. The food waits on giant aluminum sheets. Hundreds of students pick up hundreds of rectangular plastic plates, hundreds of waxed cardboard containers of homogenized milk. In just one lunch period there are thousands of bites.

It goes on: PE, assemblies, lectures, field trips, always crowds. A student excuses himself from class several times a day. Quietly closing the door behind himself he walks carefully down the hall to the boys' bathroom. He goes inside, looks at his slightly warped image in the polished steel mirror and steps into a stall. Without pulling his pants down he sits on the toilet. After a few minutes sitting there he gets up and goes back to class. Day after day his friends make not unkind fun of him for having diarrhea.

# Church and State

Everyone stood in school for the Pledge of Allegiance. It was "... to the flag of the United States of America ..." and "... one nation under God. ..." They said it every day for years.

One day a student noticed. Under God? she thought. In government class they saw a film of the Presidential inauguration. The President was sworn in with one hand resting on a Bible. The student noticed again. And when they went to observe City Court, she was struck by the witnesses' promise to tell the whole truth "so help me God." God was mixed up with everything.

The student got up to get a Coke. She pulled a quarter out and for the first time really looked at it. There they were—"Liberty" and "In God We Trust." The dime was the same. And the dollar. She put the money in the machine and the can fell into a trough below a picture of a Coke. She sat drinking and looking at her money. The nickle and the five. It was on the ten-dollar bill and the twenty. And though she'd never seen one, there was no reason to assume it wasn't on the thousand-dollar bill—"In God We Trust." She could trust a lot of something with a thousand dollars.

Later in the school year there was a woman teacher who spoke out against prayer in the classroom. She mentioned the Constitution and the law. She refused to allow prayer in her room and they tried to fire her. Some adults picketed the school on her behalf. Their signs read, "Separation of Church and State."

The student remembered her experience and wondered what the signs meant. There was no separation of Church and State. With every dollar the teacher spent she must know that, too.

# Boule Miche

The French teacher has covered the walls with posters of far-off places—the Arc de Triomphe and Notre Dame, Les Alpes du Nord and Val d'Isère, a giant blow-up of the Château Frontenac, shopping in Fort de France and beaches in Martinique covered with beautiful black people.

What's the point? Nobody here's getting out of this room, much less out of town. But one boy is dreaming of going everywhere. He's practicing *bon jour* and *je suis américain*. He loves French; it's sexy. And the French teacher, she's sexy too.

Another boy says, "Open the door and bam, there's a tiger waiting to eat you up."

"What are you talking about?" the enthusiast replies. "You always have a choice in life."

"That's right. There are two doors and you've got to open one. Behind the first there's a beautiful woman and behind the other, the tiger. No way to know which is which."

Closing his eyes the enthusiast is sitting in a cafe on the Boulevard St. Michel. Boule Miche, he calls it. His teacher taught him that. He's sitting there having a citron pressé and talking French to a beautiful girl.

"Jesus," the tiger boy says. Wouldn't he like to sit on the boulevard, too? And smell diesel fumes and a vague scent of urine washing down the street? Wouldn't he like Paris to be as familiar and good as the lover he's never going to get, the perfect one, the one who's everything? And he's older and knows what the hell is going on. And when he wakes up with a hard-on, he does it with this perfect lover and then takes a leak. And at night he turns over and touches her and feels warm and falls asleep.

"Screw the Boule Miche. And screw the French teacher, too." He thinks of the apple orchards and hops fields surrounding his town, of working after school in the fall and pruning trees in February with snow on the ground. And he works with Mexicans. And the sons of Mexicans. And when he's not there it's the same. Maybe it's true he'll never get out of town but he can get out of this room, dropping French and signing up for Spanish instead.

# And Then What?

Though the city was not large, still it was a city. One teacher who had grown up on his grandmother's dairy farm longed for life in the country. He found a book of stories about farm life in the Midwest—Iowa or North Dakota or somewhere. When he read the stories he felt like someone had thrown a cold pail of water in his face. The stories were about men who sharpened tools and built endless tiny sheds to store things in, about lonely ladies who sang to their flocks and ministers' wives who put breast milk in the parishioners' coffee, about boys who played tricks on people and about animals that were odd, like having two heads. All the stories were very short so the teacher decided to read one a day to his class. On the first day he read this one:

*Bacon*

The boys were ready to explore some more. They went off to the pig pens—a fenced area with mud wallows for the pigs to cool off in. One of the boys suggested riding the biggest pigs. This would be exciting. The boys cut some long straight willow branches. They tied a string to the end of each branch like a fishing pole and attached a piece of bacon to the end of the string. For a few minutes they all stood around looking at each other and the bacon dangling on the end of the poles. The smell was strong and the pigs started snorting and rolling their runny eyes. Then one pig snapped his head to the side and lurched up. A boy jumped on his back. The boy held the willow branch out in front of the pig who chased the bacon around the pen. Soon all the boys were on pigs chasing bacon around the pen. The pigs would make sharp turns and sometimes a boy fell off into the mud. Then one pig stopped and the other pigs came up to eat its bacon. The boy had to wave the willow branch around to keep it away from the pigs. All the pigs noticed and stopped. The boys were swinging the branches all over, slapping each other in the face and chest, but the pigs wouldn't move anymore. And so the boys finally did, dropping the bacon in the mud and running off to the irrigation ditch to wash.

A boy in the back, a city boy born and raised amid the asphalt and piped-in music, raised his hand.

"Yes?" the teacher said.

The boy was silent for several moments. He cocked his head off to one side and said, "And then what?"

The teacher was puzzled and didn't know what the student meant or what to say. But the other students understood and kept their hands down for the rest of the day.

# Unhappy

A student is unhappy sitting at her desk and unhappy standing in front of her locker. At home she is unhappy turning on a television and squeezing toothpaste out of a tube. Staring into a book, she says, "I am unhappy here, and I am unhappy there. There must be some third place to which I have never been."

She looks closely at what before has not captured her attention—the thin space between the mirror and the wall, the tiny straight river where a roadmap has been folded and refolded, the drawer filled with paper and pens. But these places are like all places.

One day sitting at her desk this student is clenching and unclenching her fist. Her painted fingernails press into her soft palm. She slows down, sees her hand open and close, lets it open and close, feels the skin tighten and go loose. When her third finger moves toward her palm its tendon rolls from the center of the knuckle to the side.

She begins to believe she is her hand, she is her finger, she is even her nail covered with polish. A teacher calls on her to speak. She can only laugh.

# Public Meeting

Last winter it cost over a million dollars to heat the school. This winter it will cost even more. The administrators have announced they can hire no new teachers. In fact, they are going to let some go. Times are changing. They're getting harder.

At the public meeting a parent suggests wood heat. Most everyone laughs. But the parent has done research. She pulls out a sheaf of papers filled with charts and graphs. She explains how much it will cost to convert the boiler room from oil to wood.

"It's not that much," a few whisper.

She reminds everyone that they live on the edge of a great forest. She knows how many trees can be cut while leaving enough for the next year. She has papers on cutting and hauling, splitting and stacking. She's talked to the maintenance men and the district engineer. Her idea is to have the students be woodcutters. The room is still. Possibly some people take her suggestions seriously.

A man questions her. "What about the girls?" he wonders. "I don't want my daughter out in the woods carrying a chainsaw. What if a tree fell? What if a choker cable wasn't set right? What if boys and girls went off together in the woods? Who is going to be responsible? My daughter isn't going to cut wood. She is in school to prepare for the future, not to live in the past."

The parent with the sheaf of papers hadn't counted on this. She was prepared to show how it could be done. Now it seems there's some issue about boys and girls and the future and the past. The administrators thank everyone for coming and adjourn the meeting. In the parking lot the two parents with opposing views find their cars parked door to door. The man has his key in the lock when he notices the woman. "You're very pretty," he says, "but you should keep out of this sort of business." Then he gets in his car and drives away.

Turning the key in her own lock the woman thinks of the contradictions in her life—driving this car, for example, or marrying a man. She'd like to resolve these contradictions and vows next time to be more prepared.

# Draft

Waking up cold a teacher goes to close a window. It drops and the sharp noise is like a shot. The teacher flattens himself against the tile floor—makes love to the floor. If it were possible to get inside that skin of tile he would. Then he wakes. The wind leaks in through the cracks around the window frame. The teacher shakes, laughs at himself, turning his head. War's over, he thinks, war's over. And he prepares his classes, giving himself to the lessons, wanting them to be good.

At lunch he relaxes by reading the paper—Government Reactivates Draft. His stomach churns. That's how they got him—the Draft. Vietnam, they said. And he served. Did his time. Got shot at. Had friends die. Came home. Wounded.

Well now he's got a son of his own starting school, learning about Sir Isaac Newton and Antarctica and the Bill of Rights. They won't get my son, the teacher vows, not like they got me.

That afternoon the teacher joins a Quaker group at the post office passing out leaflets on alternatives to registering for the Draft. He smiles and stretches out his hand to the young men, so like himself. Then he looks around. All the people in his group are old—thirty, thirty-five, forty. They are all veterans of that other Draft. All the young men are going into the building. Some show disdain—"I ain't afraid to die," some faith—"We've got to defend our country," some fear—"I don't want to go to jail."

As the day wears on the teacher feels a weight settle on him. Late in the afternoon he sits down on the concrete steps and begins to cry. Some members of his group are embarrassed. A young man going in to register stops in front of the weeping man, bends over and spits at his feet.

"It's chickenshits like you we've got to protect," the young man says. The teacher recognizes the voice and lifts his head. It's an ex-student, one the teacher especially liked. He wipes his eyes with his sleeve, smiles and reaches out a hand. The ex-student only hurries on up the steps and through the door.

# Dead Cat

Walking to school, same old stuff, and there's a dead cat in the middle of the road. Hit by a car. And the cars keep going, some around the body, some over it. At school the student writes, "It was vivid against the snow—a torn red curtain fallen on a white carpet."

"Good description," the teacher says, "very good."

But that dead cat's like me, the student thinks, then, No, not really. Some of the people in cars probably feel as bad as me. Can't blame them for the dead, they didn't hit the cat. And nobody's responsible for the invention of the automobile or the building of highways.

The student shivers in the cold walking home, jams his hands deep into his pockets, feels a rabbit's foot on a keychain. For good luck. Somebody had to kill the rabbit. Wonder if it was an old man who hit the cat. Or an executive. Or a teacher. Someone got up, got dressed and drove off to hit a cat.

"What do I care?" the student shouts to a passing motorist who can't hear him through the rolled-up windows. Confused, the motorist puts the best face on it—smiles and waves.

"What do I care?" the student shouts again. "Everything's dying!" There's no denying it. And people only exist because other things don't. Like dead cats. Damned teacher'd like that, wouldn't he. Without that dead cat on the road, we'd all disappear, go up like that, poof, in a cloud. And the student says aloud, "Poof," a cloud of breath escaping from his mouth.

# Expectations

There was a bad boy, the son of a successful lawyer. The boy's lawyer father made quite a lot of money and his mother was prominent in social circles. Both mother and father had great hopes for their son. He could be anything he wanted—a doctor or a businessman or maybe even a lawyer. He could make a lot of money. It was heartbreaking to see their son become a bad boy. They knew he drank beer and smoked marijuana, stayed out late and cruised around looking for girls. They were pretty sure he and his friends had taken cars to go joyriding. The boy's father began to think the less he knew the better.

At school the bad boy didn't go to class much. And when he did show up he'd shout obscenities at the teachers, try to proposition the female ones. There was one teacher who had a reputation for working with this sort of student. The father spoke with the principal and the computer put the bad boy in that teacher's class.

Nothing much happened differently. Only the boy signed up for a second class with the same teacher. Signed up for a third. He began to do better. Things were looking up. He graduated. Went to college. His father's hopes all began to come back. His son could become a doctor or a businessman or a lawyer. Make a lot of money.

But that's not what the boy did. He studied psychology and became a cab driver.

# Lady Driver

One teacher takes the students on a bus ride. They don't go anywhere in particular. A lady drives the bus. On the way home she pulls up to a red light next to a wrecker. The driver honks his horn at her. No one on the bus knows why, but they wave. The light turns green. A flock of starlings crosses the intersection. Their feathers shine.

Down the street the bus driver turns right. The air is filled with honking. Everyone looks out the back window. There's the wrecker. He crosses two lanes of traffic to turn behind the bus. He's up on the curb on a collision course with a stop sign. The red light on his roof shines and the wrecker miraculously misses the sign. A dog crosses the street, eyes glowing red in the light. The dog leaps, snapping at starlings.

The lady bus driver stops and the wrecker does too. The man leaps out, runs to the door and onto the bus in one bound. He demands information, says the bus clipped his mirror, yells at the lady driver, wants her name and the name of her supervisor. He wants everyone's phone number.

After riding around all day the students are expectant. Some of them shout out their phone numbers. Others shout "Back off man" and "Nobody touched your fucking mirror" and even "Hey, get off this bus or we'll beat your face in." The teacher tries to silence the students but they get louder. The wrecker too gets louder. And angrier. He shouts that he went to this high school. Everyone is up on their toes, leaning.

The lady driver turns and says, "Okay, cool it guys." The bus is quiet. The wrecker gets out and leaves. The students sit down. The teacher promises he will call and explain what happened. The lady driver takes everyone back to school.

# Little Talk

The football coach and the Poetry teacher have trouble having even a short conversation. The coach feels strange around this man who quotes Wordsworth and W. S. Merwin. He's never heard of W. S. Merwin. The Poetry teacher, for his part, doesn't go to the football games and can't remember what class it is the coach teaches.

One of the Poetry teacher's ex-students has become a famous skier. The year before, this student had broken his leg in a race in Switzerland. Some doctors believed he would never walk again. Most felt that even if he did walk he'd never ski. Now, one year later, with his bones full of pins and bolts, the student has won the silver medal in the Olympics.

The Poetry teacher knows this isn't football, but it's his only chance. Standing behind the coach in line for lunch, he speaks. "Did you hear about our ex-student? He finished second in the slalom. Won the silver medal. And only a year after that accident. The silver medal. Isn't that great?"

Picking up his knife and fork and pulling a napkin out of the dispenser, the football coach says, "Winning is awfully important," and sits down to eat.

# School Is the Same

The school gardener's mother is in a nursing home. Actually he is pretty old himself. But still in good enough shape to work. Most of the students don't even know the school has a gardener, though he has been there for many years. Some mornings now it hurts to unbend his body from bed or bend down to tend a flower.

On Saturdays he volunteers his work at the nursing home. He mows the lawn, trims hedges, prunes trees. One week he planted some nasturtium seeds outside his mother's window. He looked up into the sky and asked that she be allowed to see them bloom.

That Saturday students from Contemporary World Problems class visited the nursing home. They called the aged and infirm their adopted grandparents. The gardener jammed his spade into the earth and went to see his mother. There were some students trying to help her fix the picture on the TV. They were asking about the knick-knacks on the walls and dresser. "Who was that in this picture?" "Is that you as a young woman?" They commented on how pretty the paintings on the wall looked. The students were very nice. The gardener bought those paintings for his mother and when he brought them to her she said they looked like they weren't painted by anybody. And maybe they weren't. Maybe they have machines to reproduce Rembrandt or Van Gogh. A student was sitting in the gardener's mother's favorite chair, the chair she'd rocked him in, knitted in, talked to her husband in, passing time.

The gardener went back outside and began to work by the window. He could see the students' lips move but he couldn't tell what they said. Good. It just brought back memories. There was an apple tree by the window. He picked up the windfall apples and took them in to the students, offering to each a polished piece of fruit. All week while he and they were at school the apples lay on the ground. His mother never went out to pick any up. She couldn't. But inside the nursing home they had crafts, parties, cards, sing-a-longs, classes, plenty to do. Everyone was good to the gardener's mother. It'd be hard to find a better place to be. Not much of a chance to get lonely. And the gardener wondered why none of the students knew who he was. It occurred to him that in many of the ways of the nursing home, school is the same.

# Voice

The Art teacher went up to an English teacher feeling bad. He'd been confronted by another English teacher about his grammar in front of the students. The Art teacher wondered if maybe he should change the way he talked.

The English teacher told the story of a famous poet being interviewed for a magazine. The interviewer asked the poet what writers had influenced his work. The poet said, "You mean like Wordsworth or Yeats or Pound?"

"Yes," the interviewer said.

"None of them," the poet went on. "My biggest literary influence was my mother's voice."

And the Art teacher knew it was true. When he spoke he could hear his own mother inside his head. He used her way of pausing and letting a phrase hang there to see how it would set. When he looked in the mirror he could even see her face around the corners of his mouth. As to her grammar, that was beside the point.

That week the Art teacher began a series of paintings called "My Mother's Voice." They were large canvases with brilliant colors, somewhat dark. The pigment was built up in layers. There were no pictures of objects, but the shapes suggested them. Asleep at night, he dreamed of childhood. Awake, he brought the past back and made it something else. He was full of energy, but calm. The paintings just appeared. There was no rush. It didn't occur to him to wonder if he worked slowly or quickly. Or if the paintings were good or bad. He painted his mother's voice.

The English teacher who had confronted him saw him in the hall and said hello, asked how he was doing.

"Real good," the Art teacher said without thinking. "I'm doing real good."

# Bright Boy

A girl walks into class. A boy looks at her and his stomach does a double back flip. He thinks he may puke. He turns away, hangs on and the feeling recedes. As she approaches to smile and say hello, he prepares himself. They're friends. Once he sat down with her and tried to explain wanting her. She didn't say anything. He kept going but it came out all wrong. He sounded like he was talking about some other person who wasn't even there. Who wasn't himself. So now he tells himself he can be casual, too. Maybe she doesn't notice that his whole body is shaking.

She comes in with her boyfriend. Always her boyfriend. Later it will be her husband or lover. And they'll change. And never be him. The boy feels sick. And angry. He wants to hit a friend. Or hit the girl. Instead he takes a walk. He feels his stomach go again and doubles over to puke. It comes up. He shakes his head back and forth, "No, no, no," and tries to look up at the sky but the pain pulls him back over and he waits, staring at what he's thrown up there on the ground. The liquid is a blue-green color a little like a churning sea. Noticing it he feels a little better.

# Physical Education

The girls' PE teacher is famous for making the girls work hard to get a good grade. They have to run the mile under six minutes for an A. Or be one of the first three on the squash ladder. Or be on any varsity team.

Some angry girls decided to get back at her. They started rumors that she was a lesbian, said she looked at them funny in the shower and watched them get dressed. They suggested she had tried to seduce one girl after a track meet. The school held hearings. The girls felt bad but couldn't back out now and thought surely it would blow over. But the teacher didn't defend herself. And so she was fired. She tried but couldn't get a job in another school in town. The ex-PE teacher ended up as a receptionist in a health spa, smiling and greeting the ladies who came in to shed a few pounds.

After a few months the girls who had started the rumor felt so guilty that they went to the principal and confessed. He immediately went to the school board. They agreed that if their ex-teacher found out the girls had reneged on their story then she could sue the school and they'd be in a hopeless position. It could cost a fortune. So although facing severe budgetary constraints they decided to offer the teacher her job back and apologize.

The teacher received the school board invitation in a friendly way, said yes, and was back at work the next week. Only now there were two PE teachers, as the second one had a contract and refused to resign. So they team-taught. At first it was confusing. But as they went on it got to be fun. The two teachers arranged competitions in which each would play on one of the sides. They were both good and having one on each team improved the quality of play. Soon they began to play squash together after school. Then they began to run together before school. On weekends they went out together. Their friendship blossomed. The first time they made love they couldn't help but laugh thinking how it was they had met.

# Friends

After seven years teaching together a man and woman feel trapped. They are good friends. Both are married and know each other's spouses. On Fridays they both go drinking but not with each other. The man goes with a group of men teachers. They talk and laugh. Sometimes what they say is important but it's not everything. The man never mentions longing. The others make jokes about cunts and tits. They're all frustrated. He's frustrated. If he mentioned it, they'd make jokes about that too.

The man wants to blossom. Like if somebody had the right water and poured it over his head he'd become a flower and open right up—blossom. He'd open up for everyone, students too. Then he could really teach. But it's impossible.

So he talks to his woman teacher friend. He tells her, "I've tried to say what I mean, tried to feel what I feel. I don't know, it's not quite right. I'd give every idea I thought I had if once what came off my tongue was what I had to say." And he tells her about blossoming. She listens and talks too. Now and then one or the other of them mentions their families and spouses.

Over the years the two families have done more and more together. The children are close friends, spending the night at each others' houses.

The man begins to talk less and less. The woman says she wants to hold tight to people, wants to be good to them, tell them they matter. She touches the palm of the man's hand. He waits. She looks in his eyes without blinking.

"Yes," he says, "but with my friends it's always the same. I want to sleep with the women and I'm afraid of the men—even when I love those men."

"And me?" the woman asks, wondering if she's becoming

like a character in a novel she wouldn't be allowed to teach.

"You most of all," he answers.

They sit still. Afternoon falls to evening. They forget where they are. Outside there's a pop and the streetlights come on. The teachers blink and wake up. The streetlights hum. Funny that after seven years they have never seen each other naked. Now they can go home or drive out of town and lie down in a field. They both notice the streetlights' hum. Lovemaking can't ruin their lives. But the families, the husband and wife, will worry and wonder where the missing persons can be.

# Eternal Love

A single teacher became good friends with another woman at school. They often talked about the sanctity of marriage, the responsibility one accepts in getting married. "Till death do you part," the married woman told her single friend. "True love is eternal."

As time went by the single teacher found herself falling in love with her friend's husband, who was also a teacher but in another school. Without deciding to, the single teacher and the husband became lovers. They soon felt they couldn't live without one another. It was impossible to tell his wife, her friend, but also impossible to keep deceiving her. Things went along in a complicated and painful way until they were found out. The wife made threats. In desperation the loving couple ran away. They expected to be caught but weren't.

The only thing left to do was apply for jobs. Only they couldn't find anything in the same town. And they didn't want to do anything to draw attention to themselves. So they took jobs in two different states. At first they flew to see each other every chance they got. But as time went by they flew less and less. After some years they stopped seeing each other at all.

It was much later that they both went back to the town they'd fled. Each, without knowing the other would be there, went to visit the former wife. Shocked to see each other, they could only shake hands and sit down to talk.

# Attraction

There is a pretty sixteen-year-old girl. Her teacher finds himself sexually attracted to her. She is his height with blond hair like his. Her eyes are a pale intense green. The eyes and hair make a strange combination. Though she dresses modestly, it is in the modern style and anyone who looks must know the shape of her body.

One day the teacher, while picking out fruit at the grocery, imagines himself cupping the girl's breasts in his hands. He is surprised and instead buys bananas. Against his will the teacher is drawn to the student. He loves his wife. The student is very young. He and his wife have a good sex life. The young girl is bright and seemingly at ease. She has many friends among her peers and is popular with teachers too. The teacher admits to himself that given the chance he would make love to her. And he admits that he loves his wife.

From the way the girl talks it is clear she is a virgin. The teacher has never made love to a virgin and is frightened by his own lack of knowledge. In high school his friends made jokes about getting some from a virgin. They explained it like this: "You go to the Goodwill and buy a towel. Then you put a plastic sheet under the towel and lay both on the place where you are going to screw. When the girl's cherry pops the blood will get on the towel but even if it soaks through it can't go past the plastic sheet. Afterwards, you wrap the towel and plastic up and throw both away. Always buy your towel at the Goodwill. If you take a towel from home and don't return it, your mother will notice. But if you return it, you'll never be able to launder the blood out and your mother will notice then too."

The idea of blood being mixed up with lovemaking bothers the teacher. And he's been told the first time can be painful for a

74

woman. He doesn't want to hurt the girl. One Sunday morning he takes a bike ride and thinks about all this. His wife goes to church. He has never gone, usually choosing to read the Sunday paper.

Now he begins riding every Sunday. The ride becomes his church. He goes through a nearby canyon along a winding river. It is beautiful and he thinks of the girl. Wanting to see more of her he volunteers to chaperone a dance at school. It's crazy, all those greasy young men grabbing for her. He doesn't chaperone any more dances. Each Sunday, seeing the trees and river, he thinks of sex with his student.

In the end he invites her to go on a bike ride. His wife knows. The girl's parents know. He will keep no secrets. He tunes up the bike he originally bought for his wife. Sunday comes and she goes to church. When the girl arrives, he shows her how a ten-speed bicycle works, where to put your hands, the different positions on the handlebars, how you must keep pedaling as you shift gears, how to pick the gear you need.

Watching her body the teacher's breath is taken away. She seems to understand the bike and they set out side by side. Reaching the first hill, she leans forward to shift down but as she does so she loses her balance. Her front tire becomes caught in his rear. He tries to steer away and release the bike. Finally he does and she falls. Very slowly she rolls forward over the handlebars. Her forehead bounces off the asphalt and she lands seated motionless in the road. The teacher is terrified. He sets his bike down and runs to her. Blood is flowing from her forehead down across the side of her nose. He pulls out a handkerchief and presses it hard against the wound, assuring her that head wounds bleed profusely, that it is nothing serious, only pressure must be applied to stop the flow.

They sit down beside the road facing the river. The teacher realizes his arm is around her. His head is shaking as much as hers. She says she feels a little funny. He keeps pressing. The blood seems to stop. Now the teacher is only holding her. They sit looking at the river. He puts his index finger in his mouth, wipes spittle on it with his tongue, then smears a little of the spittle on her nose, moistening the dried blood. He shivers seeing this fluid from his body touch her. He rubs the blood hard with his handkerchief, wiping her face clean. Still he longs to make love with her. Lifting the hair carefully off her forehead, he can see the wound, a tiny hole, an almost round red bead above her eyes. Keeping his arm around her and watching the river flow by, he puts her hair back in place without saying a word.

# Speech

The Speech teacher had an affair with a student. She didn't call it an affair. He didn't either. She was the first woman he'd been with. She told her friends he was one in a million. Still it was very odd being a twenty-eight-year-old woman with a seven-teen-year-old boy. They couldn't even go out for a drink. And he was a little awkward.

They met in her Speech class. He never said much. The truth is he could hardly speak. He'd get nervous and his voice would get breathy and thin then disappear altogether. She put her hand on his throat and diaphragm, made him learn to breathe from the stomach and let the air come up in a continuous open stream. He joined the Speech Club and began to debate. They went on school trips together. He got good at debate. They began to talk.

The day it occurred to her to make love to him, she felt sick. The possible repercussions and inevitable complications seemed unbearable. All that did was slow her down. The first time they were together it was like those early Speech classes. He didn't do anything—could hardly talk. She laid her head on his stomach and told him to breathe.

It was hard to keep it a secret. She was afraid he would brag about her to his friends, then afraid she would have to tell her friends about him. She felt ashamed of her thoughts.

In the spring of his senior year the rumors got to be too much. The principal spoke with her, warned her. Teachers avoided her. Male students winked slyly at her. She began to have stomach aches. Nerves, she thought. How ironic for one who teach-es others to master their nerves so as to be able to go on. She almost laughed. Only it hurt. After three weeks the stomach aches had only gotten worse so she went to the doctor.

"Cancer," he said. "We'll do the best we can." But even then she knew and was filled with anger.

The boy tried to visit her in the hospital but she wouldn't see him, blamed herself for getting cancer, feared she wouldn't be able to speak. "Speech teacher, ha!"

So he never knew what she felt and she didn't much either. Six weeks after she entered the hospital she died. That was in May. In June he graduated from high school.

Maybe that doesn't sound real. Some people don't know what real is. One of the other teachers said it was God's punishment to her for having polluted that boy.

# Secret Love

A man teacher had fallen in love with his fifteen-year-old boy student. The man knew he had to be careful and so was very circumspect in his behavior. He dropped hints but the boy played dumb. Finally, not knowing what to do, he wrote a secret love letter to the boy. But next day in class the boy continued to play dumb. The teacher was nervous and found it hard to look at his student. During the silent reading period he noticed an envelope with his name on it shoved under his copy of the textbook. He opened it and read the note: "If you love me, tell me now." When the bell rang the teacher dismissed class.

He thought about the note and had to admit that yes the student was right. So one day in class he took a deep breath and began to explain that he was a homosexual. He said he was tired of living a lie. Most of the students were shocked. Some were angry. A few got up and walked out of class. But there was one who smiled and looked straight ahead.

# Coal Kiss

For Social Studies class the teacher organized a unit on family life. "Something about your parents," she said. One student turned in a poem called "Coal Kiss":

Coal Kiss

The fire reached out
and kissed Mother on the cheek.
She rushed to the mirror
and there on the cheek
was a black coal mark.
Shaped as lips branded.
Father walked into the house
covered head to toe with coal dust.
He put a black kiss on Mother's
other cheek. The white powder
on her black face began to fade.

When the teacher asked about this poem the student said, "It's not what I meant. I don't know where it came from."

At sixteen the student has no family. She lives alone in an apartment near school. When she finishes classes for the day she works in a restaurant until midnight. On Saturdays she works from one to six. She doesn't do much homework. She wears too much make-up and tight pink pants with shiny silver high heels. When she smiles she is beautiful.

One winter day the student and teacher leave school at the same time. "May I come to your apartment?" the teacher asks.

"Well," the student says, unsure what the teacher wants, "okay, sure." So they go. The teacher sits in an overstuffed chair that's got a blue bedspread pinned over it. The student sits on the couch. It's missing one leg. The Social Studies text replaces the missing leg. The student jokes and tries to make this life seem fine.

"Did you come to talk about school? I know I don't do all …"

"No, no," the teacher says.

So the student tells about waitressing—the funny or crazy things that happen. Like the time a fat lady in a lavender sack dress whacked the bottom of the ketchup jar and ketchup shot all over her lap. Or the time a man ordered a full dinner plate of parsley and half a lemon and ate them separately, then left. The student smiles.

The teacher is silent. Then she looks down and begins to cry. At first the student is angry because she thinks the teacher pities her and is crying at her hard sad life. But the teacher talks through the tears and it becomes obvious she is crying for herself. Feeling strange and a little silly, the student moves onto the couch, sits close to the teacher and begins to stroke her hair. It's brown and coarse and here and there are bits of gray.

# Special Education

The normal students call the Special Education students dumb. Or laugh at them. It's true some Special Ed students have thick glasses or slurred speech as though their tongues have been tied to the roof of their mouths. There's one Special Ed student whose legs seem to be attached backwards. He never seems to know where his feet will come down. Or maybe he knows exactly. They flop around like drunken birds tied to his ankles. The normal kids call the students with Down's Syndrome Mongoloids. There are kids with Muscular Dystrophy and Multiple Sclerosis, with rare blood disorders and common developmental disorders. Normal students try not to sit next to Special Ed students. Even making fun of Special Ed students gets old. As often as not they smile.

One day a Special Ed student was hit by a car while he was walking to school. He was taken to the hospital in critical condition. Every day for weeks there'd be reports about the student —whether he was improving or whether he'd need another operation. Then he died. Like that, dead. Gone. And though he was a Special Ed student, still it made a lot of people think. You're walking down the street and you get smacked by a car and you're dead.

So there was a memorial assembly at school. Almost all the students attended. The dead kid's mother and father sat up on the stage. They cried but they looked normal. The principal talked. A minister said how it was especially sad when a person died so young. Everyone felt pretty bad. Some of the normal students began to cry. The Special Ed students only smiled.

# With a Smile

On the way to the auditorium the Drama coach remembers that the door is locked. He sends a favorite student back to the room for the key. "It's in my desk somewhere," the Drama coach says. "Just look around, you'll find it."

So the student has to rummage through the teacher's stuff. In the middle drawer he comes across a notebook. It's handmade. The cover is brightly colored cloth and glued to it is a photograph of a field of turkeys. The turkeys are white as can be with long red wattles hanging from their beaks down along their necks. In the picture they're all pushed up against the fence as if they've come to get something. Thousands of white turkeys.

The student can't resist and opens the notebook. On the first page the teacher has written "All thinking is daydreaming" and "We all know what memories bring, they bring diamonds and rust."

A door slams somewhere. The student slams the notebook shut and flings it back in the drawer, pretending to be searching for the key. He waits a few moments, then opens the drawer again. The notebook rests there. He picks it up and it falls open. The student reads, "It's night, late, papers, tests, day after day, what the hell's going on? Is it worth it?"

The student's pretty sure what *it* is. Day after day. He knows about that. Again he closes the notebook and lays it back in the drawer. There on top of the desk in full view is a pile of keys. It'll be in there. He picks them all up and walks back to the auditorium where the waiting teacher greets him pleasantly, by name and with a smile.

# Cutting Wood

Along with fifteen students, the Biology teacher is cutting wood: fir and alder and madrone. They're bucking up fallen logs. Thank goodness we don't have to actually cut the trees down, the teacher thinks, though to the students he gives the impression they can do anything.

The chainsaws snarl and whir. The students argue about who gets to run them. The teacher himself hates chainsaws. He helps stack the cut rounds on the truck. He says he prefers this, but the students know he's making a sacrifice for them. They like him.

As the teacher bends to pick up a piece of fir, he notices the thick gnarled bark. It's broken in one spot, revealing an almost red sap. The layers of tissue from bark down into rings are like the different layers surrounding a cell or the layers of human flesh. The teacher finds himself thinking of the tree's flesh and thanking the tree for giving itself up to them. The teacher tries to have respect.

Then the teacher remembers his own student days in Wisconsin and cutting wood with his father. In winter they'd work till dark. Some nights his father would call him over and show him a piece of wood.

"Foxfire," Father would say. And the wood would gleam, giving off a light from somewhere deep inside. As a boy the teacher would take this glowing thing and hold it close, trying to find the source of the flame. He said he could feel the heat, the burning. His father would repeat, "Foxfire." Sometimes the boy would take the wood back to the house but once inside in the light, the fire was gone. And the wood smelled of fungus and rot.

The teacher keeps stacking, and without noticing when, begins to cry. A tear falls and its trail marks a tiny burn. The students stop working.

"What's the matter?" they ask. "Is it a wood chip in your eye? Are you hurt?"

Now, thinking of red sap, foxfire, his father and his students, the teacher can begin to stop being hurt. It's the only lesson worth teaching—except he doesn't know how. He says, "I'm alright." He keeps stacking wood.

# Zen Man

One teacher has heard there is a Japanese man living in town. Another teacher reports that he is a Zen man.

Some students have become Christians and are very zealous. They carry their copies of the Bible to school. One student, especially, some students consider a fanatic. In Speech class he gives talk after talk of warning and condemnation. He has curly hair and is nice-looking.

The teacher who has heard of the Zen man decides to invite him to her class. She hopes he will be an antidote to something that is going on which makes her uncomfortable. She calls the man up and yes he would be happy to come to her class. He does not mention Zen and the teacher forgets to tell him why he has been invited.

On the day of the meeting the teacher is nervous. It is possible some student will be offended. Some person in the community may complain. It could be anyone. The Japanese man dresses in a clean tan shirt and dark pants. He brushes his hair and washes his face in cool water. At school he speaks about his life. During World War II he was placed in a relocation camp in Arizona. It was at the camp that he met his wife. When the war ended and the Japanese were released, he stayed in Arizona working in a nursery. Then he came north, bought land and started his own flower garden. Now he and his wife work in the garden most days and sell flowers to make their living. The Japanese man says he first grew flowers in the camp. He did this secretly and in the end gave the flowers to his future wife. Then he stops speaking.

A student raises his hand. "Have you ever read the Bible?" the student asks. The teacher stays as quiet as she can.

"No," the Japanese man says.

"The Bible is the Word of God. Without it you are doomed to eternal damnation in Hell."

The Japanese man admits to little knowledge of this and asks the student to go on. He has heard that the Bible is a book of love. The teacher is surprised when the man she has heard is a Zen man makes the word "love" sound like the perfect question. The student seems confused as to how to proceed.

The one Jewish boy in class says, "Look in your Bible." The Japanese man looks at the Jew. "You know, that story about the lilies, I like that one."

"That's Matthew," the Christian student says, opening the book. Then he reads, "'Consider the lilies of the field, how they grow. They toil not, neither do they spin. . . . Take therefore no thought for the morrow, for the morrow shall take thought for the things of itself.'" The teacher and some students begin to squirm.

"That is very good," the Japanese man says. "Is there more?"

The student continues, "'Ask and it shall be given you, seek and ye shall find, knock and it shall be opened unto you. For everyone that asketh receiveth, and he that seeketh findeth, and to him that knocketh, it shall be opened.'"

The teacher, feeling she must admit her mistake, is about to stop the student and address the issue of the separation of Church and State when the Japanese man smiles.

"Very good indeed," he comments. "Whoever said that is not far from Buddhahood."

# Walk

Unaware of each other two teachers go walking in the cold late night. They have come from far to the south and are both living through their first winter in the north. Winter is for them a romantic idea more than a large heating bill and a dead battery in the car. They both love the darkness from early in the afternoon until morning. The two teach in different schools, so have never met. Their walks are the acts of solitary men.

One night about three o'clock they see each other through the falling snow. The ground is white and the sound has a softness that neither has yet been able to explain. They both have seen each other and so can't avoid meeting, however it may be tainted by shock and disdain. Both have a proprietary feeling toward the night and don't want to share it. Go away, each thinks toward the other, and passes without speaking. Another night, they inadvertently meet again. There are only so many streets and an infinite number of nights. Moreover, each is a southerner charmed by the stillness and cold.

After many nights each motions simultaneously to the other. Each has a question. Each claims to be lost, and perhaps the other can give directions. One offers a drink from the flask he carries. The other tells of the night his father died, when his mother pulled all the pots and pans and dishes and bowls down from the cupboards and threw them around the house. For days she left all these implements of domestic life strewn under her feet. The two men say good night. As they continue their walks they continue to meet. The rancor goes out of their meetings.

One night a car slowly drives behind them for two blocks, its lights shining on their fully-clothed necks and backs. It pulls up beside them and a man beckons. They make it clear they will not enter the car and the man drives away. That night they have a brief snowball fight. They say good night and go home.

Eventually they learn they have both come from the south and both are teachers. They discuss their work. In some way both feel their time at school is wasted—maybe their entire lives. Neither is married and so it is easy to get away on these eccentric late-night walks. And the winter here is so long.

On a night when they have walked longer than usual, they hear the clop of a shod horse coming from another street. They move together toward the sound. Of course it recedes, of course. But it won't disappear, the distant footfall, the imagined snow, white petals in the dark mane. Now and again the horse shakes its head. They can hear the brief clouds emerge from the nostrils.

"I never believed that stuff about God," one teacher says, "but this. . . ."

They follow the horse up and down every street in town but never see it. That night for only a moment they hold each others' hands. Then as always they say good-bye. It's hard to say if they'll come back. These walks can't go on forever. Spring is only weeks away.